D1485642

Xmas '80

I'M SORRY
I HAVEN'T A CLUE

I'M SORRY
I HAVEN'T A CLUE

Tim Brooke-Taylor, Barry Cryer, Graeme Garden,
Humphrey Lyttelton and William Rushton

Robson Books

FIRST PUBLISHED IN GREAT BRITAIN IN 1980 BY ROBSON BOOKS LTD.,
28 POLAND STREET, LONDON W1V 3DB. TEXT COPYRIGHT ©1980 TIM
BROOKE-TAYLOR, GRAEME GARDEN, BARRY CRYER, WILLIAM
RUSHTON AND HUMPHREY LYTTELTON.

The publishers acknowledge with thanks
the co-operation of the BBC.

STOP PRESS
CARTOONS BY
GRAEME GARDEN
WILLIAM RUSHTON
AND
HUMPHREY LYTTELTON
COMMENTARY ON MORNINGTON
CRESCENT BY GRAEME GARDEN
MUSIC BY COLIN SELL
DESIGNED BY HAROLD KING
PHOTO'S BY MARK EDWARDS
THANKS TO
SIMON BRETT, JOHN JUNKIN
AND JONATHAN LYNN

I'm sorry I haven't a clue.
  1. English wit and humor
  I. Brooke-Taylor, Tim
  791.44'7   PN6175

  ISBN 0-86051-108-1

All rights reserved. No part of this publication may be reproduced, stored in a retrieval
system, or transmitted in any form or by any means, electronic, mechanical, photo-
copying, recording or otherwise, without the prior permission in writing of the
publishers.

Printed in Great Britain by R. J. Acford Ltd., Chichester

DISCLAIMER

The antidote to panel games (which has for some years been annoying radio listeners) now offers the reading public the chance to enjoy wit, satire and clever parody by throwing away this book and reading something by Frank Muir instead.

When the idea of doing a book of *I'm Sorry I Haven't A Clue* first came up it was felt that there might be some problems in presenting a set of games which had been largely unsuitable for radio. But these fears proved unjustified when the book turned out to be as scrappy and unintelligible as everyone hoped.

Across 128 pages William Rushton and Tim-Brooke-Taylor take arms against a sea of Graeme Garden and Barry Cryer under the watchful eye of Humphrey Lyttelton. Their words have been retained for posterity and injudiciously re-arranged by the show's producer, Geoffrey Perkins.

Fans of the programme will find many old favourites plus quite a few new favourites. And, of course, there is the bewildering 'Mornington Crescent'. International rules are observed throughout the book – with one mark being given for a correct challenge and two marks for an incorrect one.

One final word of warning – if you are going to attempt any of these games at home please remember to pull the curtains before you start.

THE CAST

Barry Cryer

Graeme Garden

Chairperson
Humphrey Lyttelton

Tim Brooke-Taylor

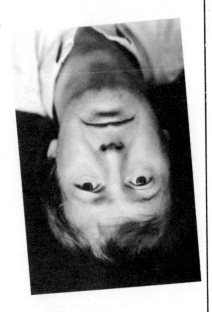

William Rushton

GOOD NEWS
BAD NEWS

HUMPH: *In this round one team has to announce a piece of good news and the others have to provide the accompanying bad news. We then go back to the first team who have to be the good news side and then over to the other team who look at the bad side, then back to the other side to look at the good side and so on until we die of apathy. Tim and Willy, we'll start with you. The good news first.*

TIM: Here is the good news: the pound is now worth $2.60.

GRAEME: **And here's the bad news: the dollar is only worth 3 cents.**

WILLY: Good news, 3 cents is worth 3 Mongolian Yaks.

BARRY: **The bad news is, the Mongolian Yak has just been taken to the vet to be devalued.**

TIM: Good news, the vet was James Herriot and he's written a book about it.

GRAEME: **The bad news is the book costs $2.60.**

HUMPH: Tim and Willy, can you start another one with the good news?

TIM: The good news is, my picture is in the paper today.

BARRY: **The bad news is, it's in the *Sun*.**

WILLY: The good news is, it's on Page 3.

GRAEME: **Bad news – he's got his back to the camera.**

TIM: The good news is, you should see Page 4.

HUMPH: Graeme, will you start one now, please, with the good news?

GRAEME: The good news is that British television is the best in the world.

TIM: **Bad news – this show's not on it.**

BARRY: The good news is, it's probably going to be.

WILLY: **Bad news – it's definitely going to be.**

GRAEME: The good news is, there will be some improvements.

TIM: **The bad news – they're changing the cast.**

BARRY: The good news – our team will be Jaqueline Bisset in a wet vest. I'll just pause for a moment.

TIM: Take your paws off.

WILLY: **The bad news is, our team will be Graeme and Barry.**

GRAEME: The good news is, the chairman will be Robert Robinson.

TIM: **The bad news is – it always bloody is.**

HUMPH: *Right, now for a musical round. I want you to sing a snatch of grand opera from a selected passage accompanied by Colin Sell at the piano. We're going to start with you, Graeme and Barry, just for a change. I want you to sing something from the collection of 'Knock, Knock' jokes.*

GRAEME: Knock, knock.
BARRY: Who's there?
GRAEME: Ammonia.
BARRY: Ammonia who?
GRAEME: Ammonia a bird in a gilded cage.

BARRY: Away, unbearably funny droll. Knock, knock.
GRAEME: All right, who's there?
BARRY: M A B it's a big horse.
GRAEME: M A B it's a big horse who?
BARRY: I thought you'd never ask.
M A B it's a big horse I'm a Londoner.

HUMPH: I'll give you eight marks for that —
minus five for interminability.

The Fotomas Library

DOUBLE FEATURES

HUMPH: *We come to the game which is called 'Double Feature' and this starts from the premise that the international film industry is broke and that new films have to be remakes of pairs of old films.*

BARRY: I am into a very exciting venture at the moment, it is a remake of a documentary called *The Jimi Hendrix Story* and that wonderful Erskine Childers' story, *The Riddle of the Sands* and it is called *Jimmy Riddle*.

GRAEME: The makers of *A Street Car Named Desire* and *Sleuth* have come up with a follow-up called *Strewth*.

TIM: The producers of *Porridge* and *A Day in the Life of Joe Egg* have got together to make *Breakfast*. They have combined *Saturday Night Fever* and *Fahrenheit 451* to make *Malaria*.

GRAEME: This is a film that's been remade out of *Half A Sixpence*, *The Dirty Dozen* and *The Exorcist* and it's *Half A Dozen Eggs*.

BARRY: Stand back for a blockbuster made from the films of recent years – *The Lord of the Flies* and *Flash Gordon* and the new film is entitled *Would You Mind Accompanying Me to the Station?*

WILLY: I have a reworking of two old movies called *Those Magnificent Men in their Little Women*.

TIM: *The Magnificent Seven* and *The Dirty Dozen* are being remade as *The Magnificently Dirty Nineteen*.

WILLY: They baulked at *Snow White* and *The Ten Commandments* but they thought they would remake *Lawrence of Arabia* with *Snow White and the Seven Dwarves*, and came up with *The Seven Pillars of Norman Wisdom*.

GRAEME: In triplicate now, adding a touch of gritty northern realism to the field of space westerns – they're going to combine *Room at the Top*, *Barbarella* and *Custer's Last Stand* and get *Rhubarb and Custard*. Not satisfied with that, they're also going to combine *Emmanuelle* and *Easy Rider* to produce *A Manual of Motor Cycle Maintenance*.

BARRY: Five films: *What Did You Do In The War, Daddy?*, *I'll Be Your Sweetheart*, *I Do, I Do*, *Be My Love*, and *Ladies Who Do*, and it's a new film called *Do Be Do Be Do*.

WILLY: This one represents a huge saving. It's *Royal Flash*, *Equus*, *Donkey's Years*, *The Four Horsemen of the Apocalypse*, *See You At The Palace*. Put it all together and it's *Racing from Windsor*.

MORNINGTON CRESCENT

HUMPH: *Once again, it's time to play that popular game 'Mornington Crescent' and, teams, the bidding must be conducted in the order F, J, O and W. You'd better jot that down – let's start now with Tim Brooke-Taylor.*

TIM: Lonsdale Road.

BARRY: Finchley Road.

TIM: You're not after me.

BARRY: I'm sorry I was too eager to jump in.

GRAEME: Finchley Road.

WILLY: St. John's Wood High Street.

BARRY: The Vale.

HUMPH: I'm surprised he didn't challenge that. Ah, Tim has a challenge.

TIM: The Vale didn't have a F, J, O or W in it, did it?

BARRY: But it doesn't have to there.

TIM: Oh, come on!

BARRY: It was above the line.

TIM: Oh, all right. Hampstead Gardens.

HUMPH: Any advance on Hampstead Gardens?

GRAEME: Parliament Hill.

TIM: I know a lot of people who live there but they don't think that.

WILLY: Play it safe. Battersea Park.

BARRY: Wimpole Street.

TIM: Upper Wimpole Street.

GRAEME: Lower Wimpole Street – Oh, it's one way – Hang on!

WILLY: Mornington Crescent.

HUMPH: Willy.

WILLY: Three J's.

HUMPH: Willy wins.

MORNINGTON CRESCENT

Would you welcome please...

The
B. B. C. Ball
R. S. V. P.

Will you carve a way through the throng for Mr and Mrs Questions and their daughter, Annie Questions.

Mr and Mrs Bennett-not-another-flaming-party-political-broadcast, and their son, Gordon Bennett-not-another-flaming-party-political-broadcast.

Throw your heads back ready to cheer Mr and Mrs Ory and their hermaphrodite child, Jack Anne Ory.

Evacuate your younger children for Mr and Mrs Britain and their son Brian F. Britain, their daughter, Ronda Britain Quiz, their illegitimate son Master Mind and their Israeli friend, Topol de Form.

Daring to follow that, Mr and Mrs ITV-for-Godsake and their chum of Sherlock Holmes's son, Watson ITV-for-Godsake.

With a burst of apathy, Mr and Mrs New and their children Gloria New, Humphrey New, Fred New, Arbuthnot New, Jessica New and little baby Jonathan New – and that is the end of the News.

Mr and Mrs Wide and their son, Nathan Wide.

Mr and Mrs Pythons-Flying-Circus and their son Andrew.

Mr and Mrs Swirled and their daughter, Tamara Swirled.

Mr and Mrs Clock-News and their daughter, Nina Clock-News.

All the way from Israel, Mr and Mrs Ook-at-Bedtime and their grandson, Abe Oook-at-Bedtime.

Mr and Mrs Service-will-be-resumed-as-soon-as-possible and their daughter. Norma Service-will-be-resumed-as-soon-as-possible.

Mr and Mrs Tin and their aggressive, nasty announcer son, News 'Bully' Tin.

An elderly lady over there, from the Your-Way family, Dawn Your-Way.

Here comes Alexandra Palace who's just laid Lord Reith.

Oh, we're in gossipy mood, are we? Alistair Cooke and Lettuce from America.

And sharing the same flight from the States, Mr and Mrs Street from America, the Streets of San Francisco.

Mr and Mrs Pie and their daughter, Meg Pie.

And Carla Television.

There's the Hertz family with their daughters, Killa and Megga.

Oh, I hear the drunken Viking, Lars Of-the-Summer-Wine.

Look, there's Ann Ouncer.

And that splendid fellow, Capital Ray Deo.

Oh, there's Freddie Night-is-Music-Night.

Oh yes, and Mandy Night-at-Eight.

Another late-comer from Scotland, Ewan The-Night-and-the-Music.

Well, ladies and gentlemen, this is where we come to the end. Mr and Mrs Sorry-I-Haven't-a-Clue and their son, from Israel, Hyam Sorry-I-Haven't-a-Clue.

The Fotomas Library

Call My Bluff

HUMPH: *We're going to play 'Call my Bluff', a game familiar to all of you who watch television. And it's played here with a slight difference. The teams are going to give me four different definitions of a word and I have to guess which one is correct. They will then tell me whether it's true or a bluff. Now the first word, teams, I want to you to define is 'hollyhocks'. Hollyhocks. Barry Cryer, will you give me your definition?*

BARRY: Hollyhocks has a very ancient derivation. It's to do with Christmas. People taken a bit short at Christmas financially were wont to hie themselves to the local pawnbroker's. Pausing only in the snow-clad street to remark on the singular occurrence that his sign had fallen down, they would rush inside and pawn something to get the money together for Christmas. This was a regular procedure, known as a holly hock. Holly hocks were what you indulged in at Christmas to get the readies together.

HUMPH: Right. Now, Willy Rushton, how about you?

WILLY: Holy hoax, in fact, Humph. These originated in the changing rooms of the Vatican City, relegated again this year. Holy hoax, as the name suggests, is a prank or trick perpetrated on a Pope – like pulling the throne out from under him as he sits down or shouting 'How's the Missus?' It's an anti-pope joke. Holy hoax.

HUMPH: O.K. Well now, Graeme, what's yours?

GRAEME: Those of you who ride will be familiar with the phrase, 'I put Black Ned over the hollyhocks.' A hollyhock is a sort of traditional fence to train jumpers – horses that jump – and the top bar of the fence has sprigs of holly nailed to it, which will prick the hocks of the horses as they leap over to make them pick their feet up and jump higher and stop them knocking the top bar of the fence off. These are hollyhocks in the riding fraternity. There was a case recently, you may have read in the paper, where a showjumper nailed hedgehogs instead of holly to the top bar of the fence: it didn't make the horses jump any higher but they had the fastest ducking hedgehogs in the land.

BARRY: Hollyhogs they were.

HUMPH: Thank you, Graeme. That leaves your definition, Tim.

TIM: This is really alco-hollyhocks. In Norway that summer I met some people who had joined Alco-Hollyhocks Anonymous. Being an alco-hollyhock is a serious complaint and I do understand that and I'm not making fun of it in any way. In Norway, however, it is made fun of, and that's why I'm bringing it into the programme.

HUMPH: Right, thank you, team. From Barry we have an object pawned at Christmas, from Willy Rushton a sort of papal prank, from Graeme Garden some rather unpleasant goings-on with horses, and from Tim the rigmarole you just heard about alco-hollyhocks. Objects pawned at Christmas – I thought that Barry faltered a little bit in the middle of his definition there. People were wont to do something – I mean, either they were or they wont, so I object to that one. I'm turning that one down. Papal prank I'd like to think about a bit more. Maybe after the programme. And Graeme's horses, I've heard of the hedgehogs stunt. Yes, but with holly, mmm; and Tim's definition – I'm going to reject that out of hand. No, no, I'm going to plump for Willy. Willy Rushton, the papal prank. Is it a bluff or true?

ALL: Show us the card.

HUMPH: Well, I lose that one. Right, teams, the next word that you have to define for me is 'launderette'. Graeme Garden?

GRAEME: Launderette is a mechanical piece of apparatus which was invented just before the French Revolution in France. It's an

22

early type of lawn-mower. It was invented by Monsieur Guillotine, after whom it was not named, and it was a sort of horizontal guillotine, which you pushed up and down the lawn to administer the coup de 'grass'.

HUMPH: Right. Tim?

TIM: Wrong. Launderette is a nineteenth century form of vehicular transport rather like a landau only it's smaller. 'Ah,' they used to cry, 'waiter, waiter, call me a launderette.' It was basically for children. A landau would be pulled by – I think – two horses. A launderette would be pulled by two rats. Actually, I lied about the horses.

HUMPH: Barry Cryer?

BARRY: Launderette. This is derived from lorgnette. Therefore, by a process of derivation, a room full of washing machines held up to the nose.

HUMPH: Right. Willy Rushton?

WILLY: It's a roomful of washing machines you don't hold up to your nose, or not with any chance of success.

HUMPH: Right. Now, let me see. Four interesting definitions there. The French lawn-mower – I'm a bit inclined towards that because I've seen one.

BARRY: You will go to those places, Humph.

HUMPH: Transport? No, no. It wouldn't work. The lorgnette, yes, I'd rather go for these French answers. Willy, yours was a roomful of machines?

WILLY: Washing machines.

HUMPH: Which you don't hold up to your nose ...

WILLY: You don't *often* hold up to your nose.

HUMPH: Ridiculous. So, yes, I'll go for that one. I was right!

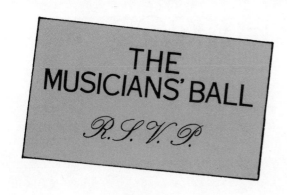

THE MUSICIANS' BALL

R.S.V.P.

HUMPH: *Musicians' Ball, please.*

Will you welcome, please, Bill Oddie and his son, Mel Oddie.

Welcome, please, from Sweden, Mr and Mrs Night-of-the-Proms and their son, Lars Night-of-the-Proms.

Will you welcome, please, Mr and Mrs Tone and their son Barry Tone and his man Dolin, who is also a bit of a liar.

Will you welcome from Ireland, please, the O'Lyns – Mr and Mrs O'Lyn and their daughter, Vi O'Lyn.

Will you welcome, please, the arrival of Mr and Mrs Harmonic Orchestra and their son, Phil Harmonic Orchestra.

And Albert Hall.

Two lunatic sisters, Clair de Lune and Mandy Lune. Accompanied by Charles Forte and his piano.

Oh, oh, will you welcome, please, Mr and Mrs Ube and their son, the pornographer, the blue Dan Ube.

That musical revolutionary, Che Mber Music.

Mr and Mrs Dante and the virginal Ann Dante and her cat, Gut.

And while we're at it, why won't you welcome, before you can think of an excuse, Mr and Mrs Raboom and their daughter, the district-attorney, Tara Raboom, D.A.; Mrs Boomsadaisy and their son Hans Boomsadaisy with Hans's niece Ann Boomsadaisy.

Mr and Mrs Uendo and their rather stupid son, dim Ian Uendo.

25

LAST EPISODES

HUMPH: *This round is called paradoxically – or perhaps prophetically – 'Last Episode'. The aim is to put the last nail in the coffin of a long-running radio or television show and close the series in one line. Tim Brooke-Taylor, you're going to be the first one. I'm going to ask you to put the finishing line for all time to* Cannon.

TIM: Mr Cannon, you're fired.

HUMPH: Willy Rushton, will you put the final line please to *Upstairs, Downstairs*.

WILLY: Rose, we're moving into a bungalow.

HUMPH: Graeme, will you put the final line to *Blue Peter* please.

GRAEME: Well, today on *Blue Peter* we're going to see what we can all get up to with a sledge hammer and half a dozen tortoises.

HUMPH: Tim Brooke-Taylor, you've got a job on your hands, we want you to put the final line to *Star Trek*.

TIM: 'Mr Spock.' 'Yes, Captain?' 'Those ears, I find them curiously attractive.'

HUMPH: Graeme Garden, the show we want you to kill off is *Gardeners' Question Time*.

GRAEME: Well, I'd like to ask the panel, how best I should feed this triffid. Down, boy, down!

HUMPH: Barry, your one is *Within These Walls.*

BARRY: Who left that door open?

HUMPH: Graeme Garden, you're going to have to put the last line to *Telford's Change.*

GRAEME: 'Good morning, doctor.' 'Good morning, Mr Telford (snip, snip) – or should I call you Dolores?'

HUMPH: Your show is *Life on Earth*, Barry.

BARRY: Tarantulas are friendly chaps. This one, for instance, is – aargh!

HUMPH: Willy, the programme that you have to put an end to is *The Money Programme.*

WILLY: Anybody got 5p for the meter?

HUMPH: We go over to Tim Brooke-Taylor now and you've got to put an end once and for all to *Tom and Jerry.*

TIM: Lawks-a-mercy, Thomas, you is a good cat. Now go and put it in the garbage can ...

HUMPH: Graeme, will you put the last sentence to *The Duchess of Duke Street*?

GRAEME: I ... I don't believe you've met Sir Charles Forte.

HUMPH: Willy Rushton, here's your series for you to finish off in one line – *Kojak.*

WILLY: This boiled egg tastes revolting.

HUMPH: Graeme Garden, I'd like you to put the finishing line to *It's a Knockout.*

GRAEME: This is Eddie Waring here in Blackpool, and it's a little bit tricky this week ... believe me, these lads can get up quite a bit of speed on these steam-rollers.

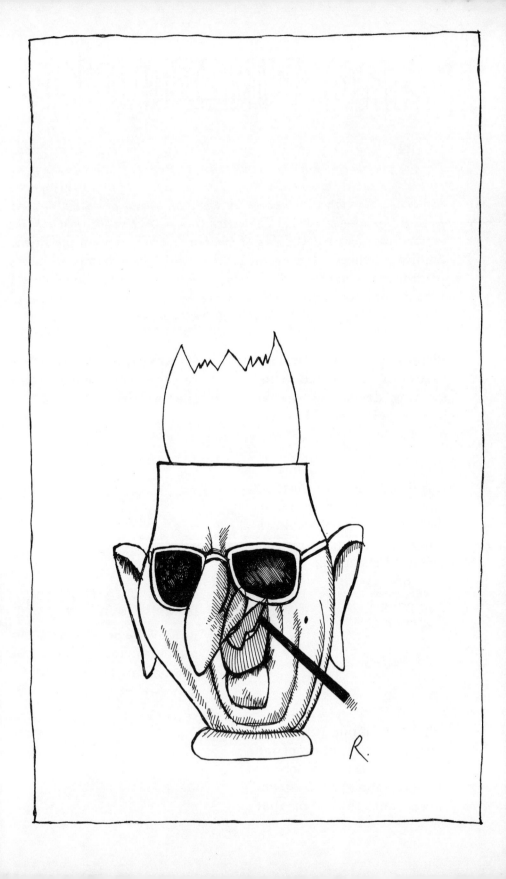

TAG WRESTLING

HUMPH: *Now, we go on to the round called 'Tag Wrestling'. In this round I'm going to give each team the pay-off of a story and I shall then start one of you off telling a story to fit your punchline. Then when I feel like it I shall press my buzzer and a member from the opposing team will have to take up the story and adapt it to suit* his *punchline. The one who reaches his punchline first wins the round. Now, Tim and Willy, your punchline is:* Whereupon the Prime Minister removed the evening dress and shook hands with the bridegroom. *Graeme and Barry, your punchline is:* 'I never thought we'd escape from that canning factory alive,' said the vet to the Chorus of Covent Garden. *Right, Tim and Willy, will you start your story now.*

Whereupon the Prime Minister removed the evening dress and shook hands with the bridegroom.

TIM: The Prime Minister wasn't feeling too well that morning. He had to go out in the evening to a ball in aid of crippled children. While the Prime Minister was getting out his evening dress –

> BUZZER

WILLY: Canning was one of our least popular prime ministers. He was forever sending gunboats to Zambesia and things of that

I never thought we'd escape from that canning factory alive.

HUMPH: Go on, Barry.

BARRY: So he went away on a holiday. It was the day of the canning factory outing –

> BUZZER

nature. Anyway, it was his daughter's wedding day, so, thrusting on his evening dress, he set off for St. Margaret's, which is next door to Westminster Abbey and slightly more posh. The young Canning was marrying Miss Canning –

⟩ BUZZER ⟨

HUMPH: Objection from Barry Cryer.

BARRY: Both the people concerned in this wedding are called Canning.

TIM: Yes, they were married.

WILLY: During the ceremony they were married.

HUMPH: Graeme Garden, will you take up the story.

GRAEME: During the ceremony the marriage took place. It was a wonderful ceremony marred only by the temporary absence of a choir, the St. Margaret's church choir having that very afternoon gone on strike for higher notes, and the only choir available as a last-minute replacement was the Chorus of Covent Garden, who couldn't be run down at the moment because they were visiting one of Canning's factories, where they were observing the humane way in which the vet was called in to put down a whale. BUZZER

TIM: So, of course, they were unable to be with us. The Prime Minister at the relevant moment in the service, when his daughter was being married to Mr Canning, suddenly realized that she was – how shall I say? – *déshabillée*. I'm only saying that because I can't think of anything else to say. BUZZER

GRAEME: Suddenly there was a bomb scare at the wedding. The vicar cried, 'Over to the canning factory, we'll be safe there.' And they all rushed into the canning factory, crammed themselves in and suddenly heard very menacing noises from outside. BUZZER

WILLY: Whereupon the Prime Minister removed the evening dress and shook hands with the bridegroom.

TELEGRAMS

HUMPH: *And now we have a game called 'Telegrams'. Quite simply, the teams are asked to send telegrams for unlikely occasions.*

GRAEME: To Yul Brynner, first night of *The King and I*:

BRYNNER.

CONGRATULATIONS.

IT'LL BE A SMASH AS SOON AS THE

WIG ARRIVES.

BARRY: To Moses:

MOSES.

YOU LEFT YOUR FLIPPERS IN THE RED SEA.

PLEASE CONTACT LIFE GUARD.

BARRY: To Nelson:

NELSON.

GOOD LUCK AT TRAFALGAR.

I'LL KEEP AN EYE OUT FOR YOU.

WILLY: To Joan Collins:

COLLINS.

STOP. STOP. STOP. STOP. STOP. STOP. STOP.

GRAEME: To Richard III:

RICHARD III.

SORRY. DICK. NO CAN DO.

WOULD YOU SETTLE FOR TWO DONKEYS?

BARRY: To the Archduke Ferdinand:

THE ARCHDUKE FERDINAND.

HAVE A GOOD HOLIDAY IN SARAJEVO.

RECOMMEND THE DRIVES.

TIM: To Abraham Lincoln:

LINCOLN.

THE SECOND HALF ISN'T AS GOOD

AS THE FIRST.

GRAEME: To General Custer:

GENERAL CUSTER.

BEST OF LUCK AT LITTLE BIG HORN.

IT'LL BE A FEATHER IN YOUR CAP.

GRAEME: To British Leyland:

BRITISH LEYLAND.

HAPPY NEW YEAR!

WHEN THE CLOCK STRIKES MIDNIGHT

DON'T COME OUT IN SYMPATHY.

TIM: To Lord Lucan:

LORD LUCAN.

ALL RIGHT. WE GIVE UP.

YOU CAN COME OUT NOW.

GRAEME: To Lord Carrington:

LORD CARRINGTON.

DID YOU KNOW MUGABE BACKWARDS

SPELLS E BA GUM?

GOOD NEWS
BAD NEWS

HUMPH: Right. Who wants to start this next one?

WILLY: I'll start because I've had a frivolous thought, Humphrey. Good news – the audience is nude.

GRAEME: **Bad news is, they've turned the lights on.**

TIM: Good news – oh look, there's Jacqueline Bisset in a wet vest.

BARRY: **Bad news – it's a trick of the light – it's Cardew Robinson.**

WILLY: Good news – he's in a wet vest.

HUMPH: Right, can anybody else come up with some good news?

WILLY: The good news is, the Queen is reading this book.

BARRY: **The bad news is, she can still have us all locked up in the tower.**

TIM: The good news is, that since the Sex Discrimination Act they've got to have female Beefeaters.

BARRY: **The bad news is that they can't join until they are over fifty-five.**

WILLY: The good news is, that's not an age it's a measurement.

HUMPH: O.K. can anybody else come up with some good news?

GRAEME: I know some good news. Any minute now Humph is going to play 'Bad Penny Blues'.

TIM: **Bad news is, he's going to play it on his teeth.**

BARRY: The good news is, he's left them at home.

WILLY: **Bad news, he's borrowing some from a lady in the second row.**

HUMPH: That one cancels out all the score so far, so we start again from scratch.

GRAEME: Here's some good news that you'll all enjoy, I got a hamster for my birthday.

39

TIM: **Bad news – fried.**

HUMPH: Willy, will you start with the good news now?

WILLY: Good news – good news. Raquel Welch came into my bedroom last night.

GRAEME: **Bad news – I wasn't there.**

TIM: Good news – I was in Brigitte Bardot's bedroom.

BARRY: **Bad news – she wasn't there.**

WILLY: Good news – Jane Fonda was.

GRAEME: **Bad news – so was Henry.**

TIM: Good news, I always fancied him.

HUMPH: I'm glad you stopped there ... stopped on the brink.

TIM: I have got some good news here. It's a braw, bricht, moonlicht nicht.

BARRY: **And the bad news is, many a mickle makes a muckle.**

WILLY: The good news is, when I've had a couple of drinks on a Saturday Glasgow belongs to me, och aye. Sorry about the walking stick.

GRAEME: **The bad news is that I never liked Welshmen.**

TIM: The good news is that David Frost has just proposed marriage.

BARRY: **The bad news is, Princess Margaret, has turned him down.**

WILLY: The good news is, Richard Nixon has accepted him on the rebound.

GRAEME: **The bad news is, Richard doesn't want children.**

TIM: The good news is, neither does David!

BARRY: **The bad news is, too late anyway!**

WILLY: The good news is, we are going to name it after the chairman.

TIM: Crawler.

GRAEME: **The bad news is, he is in fact the father.**

HUMPH: That cancels your marks out.

PARANOIA

HUMPH: *All right, teams, let's go on to a round called 'Paranoia'. In this one Team A decides that there is something wrong with Team B, and Team B have to guess what's wrong with themselves, by asking questions. Team A reply in a manner appropriate to Team B's affliction. The aim is to make members of Team B paranoid and to leave the studio twitching.*

HUMPH: Willy and Tim, you have an affliction unknown to yourselves, which you have to find out by questioning Graeme and Barry.

Willy and Tim are both nude.

HUMPH: I've just had a flash that fifty thousand people have switched their sets off. Tim and Willy, will you start the questioning please. Find out what's the matter with you.

WILLY: Has it a sexual connotation?

GRAEME: Not in your case.

BARRY: In our opinion, no.

TIM: Is it anything to do with machismo?

GRAEME: No, you keep your machismo out of this.

WILLY: Are you in any strange way jealous of it?

GRAEME: Not any more, no.

BARRY: And certainly not in any strange way.

TIM: We used to have something but we've lost it?

BARRY: Not knowing what was there in the first place, I can't speak really, but I suppose you have lost something, in a sense.

HUMPH: Willy, you'd better ask a question or they'll think you're trying to cover something up.

WILLY: It's my basic hirsuteness you're getting at again …

BARRY: Well, er, I won't be getting at it but, um …

WILLY: I'm long-haired? I shave my armpits?

BARRY: I can see that.

TIM: We've lost something. Have we lost youth?

BARRY: You will, at this rate.

HUMPH: I think it's fair to say it's something more material than that.

TIM: We've lost our wallets.

BARRY: Among other things, yes.

GRAEME: Well, if you haven't I don't know where you're keeping them.

WILLY: To put this tastefully, would we be safe serving drinks in a harem?

GRAEME: No.

BARRY: You, possibly, yes.

WILLY: Apart from that, in this game.

BARRY: Nor would you be safe frying sausages in a nudist colony, but there you go.

TIM: And it doesn't have a sexual connotation?

BARRY: Stay away from electric fans.

WILLY: Is there a measurement involved?

HUMPH: No, they're not going to get it, so you'd better tell them what they are. Now, Tim and Willy, it's your turn again.

Tim is not here.

HUMPH: Right, start the questions.

TIM: Does it apply to both of us? (*Silence*) Oh, it's going to get bitter, this.

WILLY: Do I have it more often than Tim?

GRAEME: What's that got to do with it?

BARRY: Stick to the game. Well, Willy, you're winning in this situation in which you've found yourselves, I would have said.

WILLY: Ah! It's not hirsuteness.

HUMPH: Tim has a question?

TIM: Were we misled by the fact that both of us are different on this? (*Silence*) Is our diction bad? (*Silence*) I've heard of clues, but silence ...

BARRY: Come on, Willy.

TIM: Would I be dumb by any chance? (*Silence*) Am I silent? (*Silence*)

44

HUMPH: I think you'd better take up the questioning, Willy, if you could. Tim has intimated that he has the answer by getting up and leaving. Tim is not here.

Son of DOUBLE FEATURES

TIM: The film industry are plundering the stage and they're now doing a film taking *Otherwise Engaged* and *The Bed Before Yesterday* and *No Sex, Please, We're British*, and it's to be called *No More Sex, Please, We're Otherwise Engaged in the Bed Before Yesterday*.

BARRY: I've got a four-hander. I have combined *Butterfield 8* with *M*A*S*H* and *The Battleship Potemkin* and *The Desperadoes* and I've got *Buttered Mashed Potato*.

WILLY: *One Flew Over The Cuckoo's Nest, King Kong, Murder at the Vicarage* and they just called it *What the Hell Was That in a Dog Collar?*

BARRY: I've just had a whisper that there's a plan to combine *Hair* and *Dry Rot* in a film called *Dandruff*.

TIM: The makers of *The Texas Chain Saw Massacre* and *Animal Farm* have got together to produce *Bacon at Thirty Pence a Pound*.

GRAEME: Here's a multi-media triple bill: they're remaking *Von Ryan's Express*, *Evita* and *Chalk and Cheese* to make *Von Ryvita and Cheese*.

BARRY: This is a remake of two very successful old films, *The Roman Spring of Mrs Stone*, and *Meet Me In St. Louis*. It's called *Stone Me*.

WILLY: *Guess Who's Coming to Dinner, Sunday, Bloody Sunday, Oliver*, and *Read All About It*, and it's called *Bloody Oliver Reed Is Coming to Dinner, Sunday*.

WILLY: Well, it's a very old movie called *My Darling Clementine* which is being tied into *Kentucky Fried Movie* to produce *The Clement Fried Story*.

THE DRUNKS' BALL
R.S.V.P.

Mr and Mrs Tasanute and their son, Piers. And his parrot, Litic.

Mr and Mrs Notheroneplease and their son, Oliver Notheroneplease.

All the way from South America, Mr and Mrs Over the Eight and their son, Juan Over the Eight.

Oh, there is Duncan Disorderly with Wild Bill Hiccup.

Mr and Mrs Sot and their daughter who is still waiting outside in the cab, known to us all as In-toxi-Kate.

And of course a distinguished visitor from the Court of King Arthur, Sir Osis of the Liver.

Not to mention Mr and Mrs Policello and their daughter, Val Policello.

Mr and Mrs Tonic and their lovely daughter, Jean Ann Tonic.

Please welcome Arthur Bitter and his meek daughter, mild Ann Bitter.

Camp 'arry and his caustic friend, dry Ginger.

And a warm welcome, please, all the way from sunny Italy, the Teeny family, Mr and Mrs Teeny and their lovely mother, sweet Ma Teeny.

All the way from Scotland, Angus Dura Bitters.

Those enthusiastic clairvoyants, Mr and Mrs Dry Sherry, and their medium, Dry Sherry.

From Sweden, Mr and Mrs Tortoise and their son, Lars Tortoise-Please.

Find your glasses for Mr and Mrs Knees Pale, and their son, Wat.

49

Word for Word

HUMPH: *We go on now to the game 'Word for Word' and in this round one of the members of the team says a word and his partner must say another word totally unconnected with the first, and so on. The other team must try to prove a connection to my satisfaction (which is very difficult). I'll feed you with the first word, then, and we'll start with Barry Cryer. The word is 'sturgeon'.*

BARRY: Flint.

GRAEME: Zither. (BUZZER)

WILLY: There is a well known statue of a sturgeon in Vienna, the home of the zither.

TIM: That is true.

WILLY: The third man, Orson Welles, hid behind it.

HUMPH: I will have to give the mark, and there is only one mark, and I will have to give it to Tim and Willy and go on to Tim Brooke-Taylor. 'Atmosphere'.

TIM: Egg.

WILLY: Coypu.

TIM: Belt.

WILLY: Tool-box.

TIM: Frock.

WILLY: Greed.

TIM: Polo.

WILLY: Anathema.

TIM: Hermaphrodite. (BUZZER)

BARRY: Hermaphrodites are anathema to me, it is purely a subjective, personal reaction, but I have never got together with any of them at any one time – there is a connection to me, Humph, personally.

HUMPH: It is your turn, Willy Rushton, to start. Start with the word 'boot'.

WILLY: Drainage.

TIM: Bi-lingual. (BUZZER)

GRAEME: Drainage and bi-lingual, neither of them start with a 'V'.

HUMPH: Ah. Correct. Now Tim, your word is 'Button'.

TIM: Clog.

WILLY: Garbage.

TIM: Daffodils.

WILLY: Booze.

TIM: Surgical belt.

WILLY: Pump.

TIM: Gerbil.

WILLY: Bottle.

HUMPH: I have a challenge there from Barry.

BARRY: Making a gerbil in a bottle is a very old pastime. It replaced ships years ago.

WILLY: I knew there was a connection.

HUMPH: I've got one on my mantelpiece. Willy, you are going to start now, your word is 'Fly'.

WILLY: Kneecaps.

TIM: Ashtray.

WILLY: Barometer.

TIM: Bell.

WILLY: Earplug.

HUMPH: Challenge from Graeme Garden.

GRAEME: I think earplug and bell definitely have a connection. If you were assailed by very noisy earplugs you'd stuff a pair of bells in your ear …

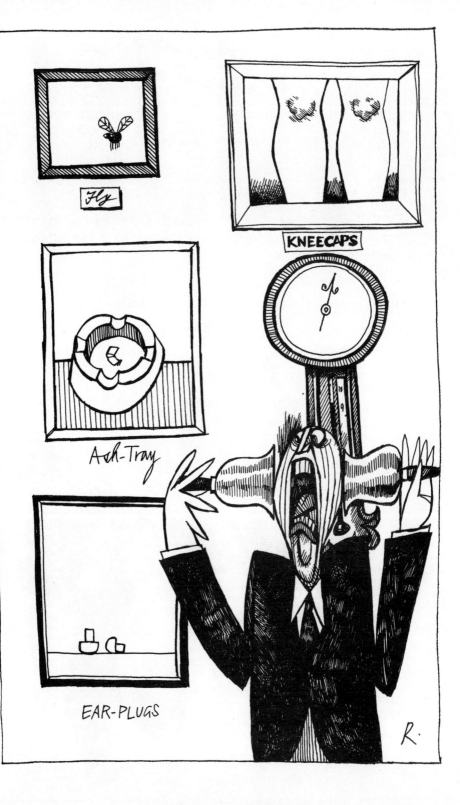

HUMPH: We'll have straight rules.

WILLY: Right, em ... straight rules, is it? Don't you get excited, I've got this one pretty well sorted out. I'm warning you. Bloomsbury Square.

TIM: Oh yes, you have.

BARRY: Euston Square.

TIM: Oh, that blew that one, didn't it? Russell Square it's got to be.

GRAEME: What?

TIM: Russell Square.

BARRY: Three squares, oh, Humph. Bayswater Road.

WILLY: Mornington Crescent, you fool, you fool.

BARRY: Why?

TIM: Three squares ...

BARRY: Bayswater Road.

HUMPH: 'Tisn't.

TIM: Not after three squares.

WILLY: Oh deary me – his mind's going.

HUMPH: If we had the anti-clockwise rule you might have got away with it, but not otherwise. O.K. Willy wins.

BARRY: I have never been accused of being a good loser.

HUMPH: Our Mornington Crescent champion for this week. Sorry, you said something, Barry?

BARRY: I said I could never be accused of being a good loser. I just didn't agree with that.

MIS_SED HIT_S

HUMPH: *Let's go on to a round called 'Missed Hits' – lesser known versions of popular plays, films and novels.*

BARRY: *Bed Knobs and Hoovers, Guess Who's Coming for a Sandwich, Anne of 999 Days.*

TIM: *Journey to the Centre of the Room, Champion, the Wonder Slug, Gone with the Flatulence, Tarzan, Lord of the Upper Fifth, Reasonable Expectations, Sinbad and the Forty People who might understandably have done something a little bit wrong if their environment was against them, The King and Me, Kramer versus Maskell*[1].

GRAEME: *Krakatoa East of Sidcup, Bonnie and Claude, The Thirty-Eight Steps, Tuesday, Bloody Tuesday, Star Trek – The Colour Slide, Rosencrantz and Guildenstern are Poorly.*

WILLY: *The Odeon Strikes Back, Dial F For Murder.*

SUITCASES

HUMPH: *Now for a game called 'Suitcases'. The teams are going on holiday, and everything they pack in their suitcase must begin with the same letter. Opponents may challenge if they think any of the objects won't fit into a suitcase. The defending team must then explain how they intend to cram it in. Right now, Tim and Willy, you're going to pack the first suitcase. Yours begins with D.*

TIM: DRAWING PIN.

WILLY: DIRIGIBLE. (BUZZER) Deflated.

GRAEME: I'll accept that.

TIM: DONKEY.

WILLY: DIANA DORS. (BUZZER)

HUMPH: Challenge from Graeme.

GRAEME: Deflated or inflated?

WILLY: Which – the donkey or Diana Dors?

GRAEME: Who's counting? And what a great act they were.

HUMPH: No, I don't accept that challenge. You can continue.

TIM: DRINKS, DRAWBRIDGE.

WILLY: ENTEROVIAFORM. (BUZZER)

TIM: Or as it is now called, DENTEROVIAFORM.

HUMPH: Challenge from Graeme Garden.

GRAEME: No. I withdraw the challenge. Tim corrected it. He pulled Willy's chestnuts from the fire just in time.

HUMPH: I'm not interested in that. Go on, Willy.

WILLY: DUNGAREES. DRAWBRIDGES. (BUZZER)

BARRY: Repetition – oh, it's the wrong programme.

HUMPH: I'll accept it, though – that was repetition there. A correct challenge from Barry Cryer. Now, Graeme and Barry, you're going to pack your suitcase with objects beginning with P.

GRAEME: PENCIL.

BARRY: PETUNIAS.

58

GRAEME: PILLOW SLIP.

BARRY: PARKA.

GRAEME: PARASOL.

BARRY: NICHOLAS PARSONS. (BUZZER)

HUMPH: Tim Brooke-Taylor has challenged you.

TIM: Nicholas Parsons and Sir Peter Parker both in the suitcase together – there isn't room. It may be fun, but there isn't room.

HUMPH: Justify it, would you please?

GRAEME: Who wouldn't want to ram Nicholas Parsons into a suitcase?

TIM: Yes, I'll accept that.

WILLY: Would you want to take him on holiday?

BARRY: Only if he didn't want to go.

TIM: I accept that, too.

HUMPH: I think, Tim and Willy, you'd better start packing another suitcase with objects beginning with Q.

WILLY: QUEEN. (BUZZER)

GRAEME: Is that a reigning queen or a *Harper's and Queen*?

BARRY: It could be a chess queen.

HUMPH: That objection is over-ruled instantly, so would you carry on, Tim and Willy.

TIM: A QUEEN.

GRAEME: What?

TIM: That's the other sort of queen.

WILLY: QUILL. (BUZZER)

HUMPH: Challenge from Barry Cryer.

BARRY: Repetition again, Humph. Two queens in a suitcase.

HUMPH: The challenge is too late, we've gone on to quill.

TIM: QUINK INK.

WILLY: QUANGO. (BUZZER)

HUMPH: There's a challenge from Graeme Garden.

GRAEME: You wouldn't get a quango in a suitcase.

WILLY: It's a very small quango. (BUZZER)

HUMPH: O.K., Tim and Willy, continue.

TIM: A QUARTER POUND OF MINCE. And a QUARTER POUND OF HUMBUGS.

WILLY: The top row of my typewriter, the QWERTYUP. A QUANTITY OF SOCKS.

TIM: A QUANTITY SURVEYOR.

WILLY: Someone to look at the socks.

TIM: A Q. (BUZZER)

HUMPH: A challenge from Barry Cryer.

BARRY: Cue – in the billiard/snooker sense, yes. But a queue of persons, surely not.

WILLY: A little model queue made by Airfix – little people waiting for a Hornby train.

BARRY: I withdraw my objection.

WILLY: A QUADRILLE. Just the instructions on how to do it in case four of us get together and can't think of anything else to do.

TIM: A QUIRE OF PAPER.

WILLY: A spare QUARTER-DECK.

TIM: A CUNARD LINER.

WILLY: Cunard doesn't begin with Q.

TIM: Doesn't it? Oh. QE2 does, though. (BUZZER) A model.

HUMPH: O.K., carry on.

TIM: All those people out there who play Scrabble will be going, 'Why doesn't he say –?' (BUZZER)

HUMPH: Graeme Garden?

GRAEME: Why doesn't he say it?

HUMPH: Yes, I'll uphold that. So you win that round. We'll ask Graeme and Barry to pack a suitcase now beginning with the letter J.

BARRY: A JAY BIRD – easily accommodated in a suitcase.

GRAEME: Some JUICE. (BUZZER)

HUMPH: There's a challenge there from Willy Rushton.

WILLY: How many Jews?

BARRY: Four, but to you, three. JANGLE BOX – it's small, portable, easy –

HUMPH: Don't justify it unless you get challenged please, or we'll be here all day.

GRAEME: JUG. (BUZZER)

HUMPH: There's a challenge. Tim Brooke-Taylor?

TIM: I just wanted to hear him justify jangle box again.

HUMPH: Objection over-ruled, carry on.

BARRY: JACARANDA.

GRAEME: JIGSAW.

BARRY: JULEP. Mint, of that ilk.

GRAEME: JAPE BOOK.

BARRY: JUMBO PACKET OF SAFETY PINS.

GRAEME: JIGSAW (BUZZER)

HUMPH: Challenge from Tim Brooke-Taylor.

TIM: Two jigsaws – they can't be allowed.

WILLY: Well, our two queens can play them.

HUMPH: I uphold that.

TIM: Whose side are you on?

HUMPH: In point of fact I didn't tell you 'cause I wanted you to carry on but you were disqualified minutes ago. If you pack a jacaranda you're infringing every customs regulation the world over. And you will be reported.

The Criminals' Ball
R.S.V.P.

All the way from Sweden, Mr and Mrs Eny and their son Lars Eny.

Mr and Mrs Meanour and their foul daughter, Diana, who is known as the foul Miss D. Meanour. Closely followed by Mr and Mrs Curity-Wing and their daughter, Topsy Curity-Wing.

All the way from Australasia I have Mr and Mrs Krobbery and their son, Ben Krobbery.

And from Italy welcome, welcome our EEC brothers and sisters, Mr and Mrs Blimey-it's-a-Fair-Cop-and-no-Mistake and their Mafia daughter, Cora Blimey-it's-a-Fair-Cop-and-no-Mistake.

Mr and Mrs Harm and their Greek singer son, Grivas Bo Diddly Harm.

And all the way from France that famous courtesan Madame Fifi escorted by her lovers, the Count of Monte Cristo, the Count of Aragon, the Count of Versailles, and she would like fifteen other similar counts to be taken into consideration.

Mr and Mrs Cused and their daughter, Thea Cused.

Oh there's Ma Kurst and her husband, Pa Kurst.

Mr and Mrs Ness and their amusing son, Wit Ness.

Dr and Mrs Bird and their ill eagle.

Mr and Mrs Decent-Exposure and their son, Ian Decent-Exposure.

Oh, and there's Mal Practice.

Sound Charades

HUMPH: *This is a game called 'Sound Charades'. One team will act out a film, book or play and the other team has the enviable task of guessing what the hell they were talking about. Right! Tim and Willy, will you tell the opposition whether it's a film, a book or what?*

WILLY: It's a film.

TIM: Two words.

WILLY: We're doing it all in one.

HUMPH: Right.

TIM (*falsetto*): Oh Carlo, what do I do next?

WILLY: Eh Sophia, I wanna you to pucker the lips when I shout the action.

GRAEME: That's *Law and Order*.

WILLY: Close.

GRAEME: Loren Order I thought was pretty good, but I'm alone. *Apocalypse Now*.

HUMPH: Tim and Willy.

TIM: Three words.

WILLY: And a film.

TIM: To our knowledge it's only a film.

HUMPH: Go ahead.

TIM: (*falsetto again*) Tara then. Well, eh, I'll be off then.

WILLY: Yes.

TIM: Well, *arrivederci*.

WILLY: Yes, yes.

TIM: *Au revoir.*

WILLY: Yes, certainly, certainly.

TIM: Well then, toodle pip.

WILLY: I think you've got my trousers on, actually. It's irrelevant, Barry, that's *en passant*.

TIM: Well, I'd better make myself scarce then.

WILLY: Yes.

TIM: Do you want my phone number?

WILLY: No.

TIM: Well, tara then.

WILLY: Yes.

TIM: I'll push along.

WILLY: Push away.

GRAEME: Right, so easy, it was a bit embarrassing. It's *The Big Sleep*.

BARRY: Well, it was for us, anyway.

GRAEME: *The Goodbye Girl*.

HUMPH: Yes.

HUMPH: Graeme and Barry, you are going to do another one now, and this one I happen to know is a film and a book as well.

GRAEME: The play was called something different, just to help you.

HUMPH: It might have been a TV show too, mightn't it?

BARRY: And it was a great Chinese meal!

TIM: How many letters?

GRAEME: How many letters? We don't get any mail on this programme.

HUMPH: How many words?

GRAEME: Three, including an article.

HUMPH: O.K., let's have your charade.

GRAEME: Now I am going to give all of you six of the best.

BARRY: You are not caning me, sir.

GRAEME: (*different voice displaying his versatility*) Oh no, don't come near me with that cane.

BARRY: I'll have none of that cane, sir, you'll have a mutiny on your hands.

GRAEME: Whatever you do, do not cane us mutineers.

BARRY: We mutineers say no more cane.

TIM: It is obviously not *The Caine Mutiny*.

HUMPH: In fact it is.

TIM: Oh.

WILLY: I say, Duchess, would you like some more marijuana on your rissoles?

TIM: Cheers. Actually, I'd like a little cocaine shredded on it. I'm going to Ascot for the grass, you know. Can I stop now?

BARRY: I was there when it happened but I don't know what it was called.

GRAEME: I think it's *High Society*. Book and film, and it's four words. We're doing it all of a piece.

BARRY: All of a piece as is our wont.

GRAEME: What's that chap doing behind that beach hut?

WILLY: *Riddle of the Sands*.

GRAEME: We've got one more.

TIM: Have you no shame?

GRAEME: It's a ballet. So ... sound effects. Ching ching ... Good morning, sir. I'd like to complain about the sofa and two armchairs that I bought from you last week and I've brought back to the shop now.

BARRY: Well really, sir, what seems to be wrong with them?

GRAEME: You try sitting on them, matey.

WILLY: *The Rite of Spring* or, conversely, the *Nutcracker Suite*.

BLUES

HUMPH: *This is the round we call 'Blues'. One team gives the other one a topic for a blues and the other team then improvises a blues on the spur of the moment, accompanied by Colin Bell. Tim and Willy, you're going to do the first one – so I'm going to ask Graeme Garden to give you a subject.*

GRAEME: I thought of ITV.

BARRY: And I thought of ITV 2. So we thought of 'The ITV 2 Blues'. (MUSIC)

WILLY: I woke up this morning.

TIM: I turned on the new cultural ITV Two.

WILLY: I heard the announcer announcing, as I sat down on the loo.

TIM: The next programme's going to be Ingmar Bergman's *Crossroads*.

WILLY: Then there's Jean-Luc Godard's *Coronation Rue*.

HUMPH: Well, judging from that applause we'll give you six marks. Right, Graeme and Barry, it's your turn to sing a blues. And Tim and Willy, can you give them a subject, please?

TIM: As I see it, it's 'The Optician's Blues'. (MUSIC)

BARRY: Woke up this morning in a state of extreme perturbation.

GRAEME: I heard my mother-in-law was coming to stay and she is my ... revelation.

BARRY: Yes, she is ... give them a choice. She's got one glass eye – you can tell which one it is because it's the one with a spark of humanity in it.

GRAEME: I didn't know she had a glass eye – till one day it came out in the course of conversation.

TIM: 'The Cold in the Nose Blues'. (MUSIC)

GRAEME AND BARRY: Woke up this morning with a terrible cold, you bet.
I went to my doctor and, you know, I purposely didn't go to see my vet.
He said, 'Drink a large whisky after a hot bath.'
I said, 'I ain't drunk this hot bath yet.'

TIM: 'The Poultry Farmer's Blues'.

BARRY AND GRAEME: Woke up this morning, then I drove off down a lonely country track ...
I ran over a cockerel and I cried out, 'Alas and alack!'
So I told the farmer's wife, 'I would like to replace your cockerel.'
She said, 'Please yourself, the hens are round the back.'

HUMPH: And now I'm going to introduce a new facet to the game, because I am going to impose a penalty of forty marks for anyone who uses the words 'Up', 'Morning', 'Woke' or 'This' (laughs). O.K., Barry and Graeme, will you give Tim and Willy their subject?

71

BARRY: Yes, we would like to hear their 'Tory Party Blues'. (MUSIC)

TIM AND WILLY: I aroused myself just after sunrise and found something heavy hanging on my brow, oh yeah!
It was Mrs Thatcher. 'Get off,' I cried, 'you daft old cow.'
But one thing you've got to say about Maggie Thatcher ...
She was only a grocer's daughter, but she taught Sir Geoffrey Howe.

HUMPH: Right, Tim and Willy, you give Barry and Graeme a subject please for their blues.

TIM: 'The Flying Saucer Blues'. (MUSIC)

BARRY AND GRAEME: I roused myself earlier today and something happened that was quite unique,
I saw two flies playing football in a saucer and I heard one of them speak.
He said, 'Take it easy, Charlie, remember we're playing in the cup next week.'
Sorry, we thought you said 'Fly-in Saucer Blues'.

HUMPH: That was so brilliant on both sides that I wouldn't dream of awarding any marks either way.

THE OPTICIAN'S BLUES.

Arr. Colin Sell:

UNTIL ONE DAY IT CAME OUT IN THE COURSE OF CON-VERS-

(a tempo)

-A-TION.

OH - YEAH!

f

Rall... ff

© 1980 Colin Sell

TAG WRESTLING

HUMPH: Tim and Willy, your punchline is: '*So the hedgehog pounced ... and custard flooded the brewery.*' Barry and Graeme, yours coming up. '*The choirboy went peep, peep, but the cactus wobbled as they sat.*' Tim Brooke-Taylor, start this off.

So the hedgehog pounced ... and custard flooded the brewery.

The choir boy went peep peep, but the cactus wobbled as they sat.

TIM: Chief Inspector Hodgkinson, known as Hedgehog of the Yard was strolling along outside Buckingham Palace when he suddenly heard sounds of merriment. It was Prince Edward's birthday party. BUZZER

HUMPH: Graeme Garden?

GRAEME: Prince Edward was in fact a member of the local choir, the Buckingham Palace Choir and was known as a choirboy. He was deeply upset to learn of the recent demise of Hedgehog of the Yard as he knew him well and attended the funeral and shortly after that ... went on a tour of America ... BUZZER

HUMPH: It's over to Willy Rushton.

WILLY: Where indeed they went to Milwaukee where

the brewers were going quite berserk, because it was during Prohibition. So the brewers naturally turned to producing various forms of other liquid which they could make in the same vats, for instance, custard . . .

BUZZER

HUMPH: Barry Cryer?

TIM: Which they make when they wish to go for a short holiday. While on holiday one of these Indians happened to get the film rights of a British film about an ex-Scotland Yard man called Hedgehog but it had to be set in America, and of course for the American audience where better than Milwaukee where the brewers produce custard. So the film starts . . .

BUZZER

BARRY: An interesting side-line but that's having nothing to do with this story. They were taken out on a day excursion to the desert and Prince Edward known, of course, as the choirboy, was invited to sing with the rest of the choir in the desert. Now there's a quaint old tradition in the Mojave Desert among the Indians of the Mojave Desert, their cry of peep, peep . . .

BUZZER

HUMPH: Tim?

GRAEME: 'I have this great idea, boss, Cactus Custard.' 'Tell me all about it as soon as these choirboys have left the room,' said the boss of the brewery. 'They are about to demonstrate the strange cry of the Indians of the Mojave Desert.' *BUZZER*

WILLY: Indian choirboys being wholly irrelevant to the film, the producers say we cannot have more of this. But I do like the inspector, he is excellent – and I like the references to Prohibition ... those you will keep in and the custard makes for a wonderful dénouement. I can almost imagine the dénouement now with the inspector suddenly ...

BUZZER

BARRY: Suddenly the head of the studio walked in saying, 'I have my own ideas on this story, we build up to a climax in the desert where you have this lone choirboy in the rays of the setting sun ... *BUZZER*

TIM: 'What am I talking about?' he said, 'I'm having one of my fits again. What I meant to say was the final dénouement of this is when the brewery must be destroyed. And the Hedge-hog comes in to solve ...'

BUZZER

GRAEME: Then a choirboy played by Doris Day comes in with a motor horn and finds this cactus. *BUZZER*

WILLY: 'Doris Day could play the inspector,' said the producer, 'or indeed she could play the custard. Howard Keel possibly doing a brewery number. Now there's this huge final scene with the Busby Berkeley, it's the brewery, there's the yellowness of the custard and there's the magnificent final scene when the hedgehog in all his glory ...'

BUZZER →

BARRY: 'Suddenly observes the ancient custom of cactus-sitting taking place before him.' BUZZER

TIM: 'The hedgehog turns round in a wild moment and at that moment he decides to destroy the brewery and the hedgehog pounces and custard floods the brewery.'

The Vets' Ball

HUMPH: *I ask you to announce your late arrivals for The Vets' Ball. An open contest, anyone can start.*

Will you welcome, please, Mr and Mrs Yancats and their son, Perce Yancats.

Will you welcome, please, before anybody else brings them in, Mr and Mrs Malhusbandry and their daughter, Annie Malhusbandry.

Mr and Mrs Bees and their twin sons, Wally Bees and Ray Bees. Also from Australasia, Mr and Mrs Guru and their son Ken Guru. Mr and Mrs Nian and their son from Britain, Pommy Ray Nian, and his duck, Bill Platypus.

And also from Australia, Mr and Mrs Matosis and their daughter, Mitzi Matosis.

(We have a lot to blame the colonies for.)

And her chum, Anne Thrax.

Welcome, please, the widow Mrs Clarethisanimalunfittorun and her daughter, Ida Clarethisanimalunfittorun and from Ruislip, Mr and Mrs Pottomus and their drop-out son, Hippy Pottomus.

Oh, there's George Shearing and his wife, Sheep.

Mr and Mrs Wobbles and their dog, the Collie Wobbles.

Mr and Mrs Satian and their son Al.

And Mr and Mrs Russell Terrier and their son Jack!

Mr and Mrs Hastwohumps – as-opposed-to-a-camel – and their musician son, Drummer Derry Hastwohumps – as-opposed-to-a-camel.

Be upstanding, please, for Her Worship the mare.

MISLEADING ADVICE

HUMPH: *Misleading advice which you might give to a tourist, along the lines of 'Have you tried the echo in the Reading Room of the British Museum?'*

WILLY: *If you have kids, don't miss the Battersea Fun Fair.*

TIM: The all-night chemist in Morden is very handy. Most tube trains will stop if you flag them down.

BARRY: You must try the open air loos in Trafalgar Square. When the organ starts in Westminster Abbey, the first couple on the dance floor wins a prize.

GRAEME: *Help yourself to the free gifts in Harrods. Hire a donkey and join in Trooping the Colour.*

BARRY: *London policemen like to be addressed as 'Tit Face'.*

TIM: For some extraordinary reason most of the guide books leave out Cricklewood. You can go by car if you like, but it's not a long walk to Stratford.

Mr and Mrs Bus and their rather oblique daughter Rhom, and all the way from Liverpool, their singing daughter Cilla Bus.

Mr and Mrs Bra and their son Algy.

All the way from sunny Greece, Mr and Mrs Beta-gammadelta-epsilon-zeta-eta-theta, and their son, Alfie Betagammadelta ...

Mr and Mrs Nastic-Display-in-the-Playground-at-Three and their son, Jim Nastic-Display-in-the-Playground-at-Three.

Mr and Mrs Tation and their son Dick.

Mr and Mrs Trons-a-bit-of-a-goer and their lovely daughter May Trons-a-bit-of-a-goer.

Will you line up in rank to welcome Mr and Mrs Education with their son, Private Education and his friend, Corporal Punishment.

Mr and Mrs Matics and their rather posh daughter, Martha Matics.

Mr and Mrs Present and their children, Smith Present and Wilkinson Present.

Mr and Mrs Masters-Study and their son, Ed Masters-Study.

Mr and Mrs Bun and their pyromaniac son, known as the Bun's son 'Burner'.

Mr and Mrs Nometry and their horse, Trigger.

Mr and Mrs Terchips and their daughter, Miss Terchips.

Mr and Mrs Cate-of-Education and their distinguished military son, General Sir Tiffy Cate-of-Education.

The Return of the Revenge of Son of DOUBLE FEATURES

GRAEME: There is a remake of *Frankenstein*, *Mary Queen of Scots*, *The Return from the Grave* and *Journey's End* and they're going to call it *Frank and Mary from Gravesend*. Not to mention the remake of *William Tell*, *Snow White* and *The Wrong Arm of the Law*, which is being remade as *William Whitelaw*.

Burst into tears amidst
ALIEN CORN!*
*(NOT ALAN COREN)

WILLIAM WHITELAW!

Remember— In Space
No-one can hear
you yawn

TIM: *The Man Who Knew Too Much* and *The Shoes of the Fisherman*, which is being called *Clever Clogs*.

GRAEME: They are remaking *Get Carter* and *Ben Hur* and they are calling it *Get Her*.

TIM: Stephen Sondheim is presenting a new musical based on *Side by Side by Sondheim* and *A Little Night Music* and it is called *A Little Bit on the Side*.

BARRY: A conglomeration, Humph, they are combining the best elements of *Nicholas and Alexandra* and *Bob and Carol and Ted and Alice* and *Pete and Tilli* and calling it *We Must Get a Larger Bed*.

WILLY: You may remember that old Peter Finch classic of the outback, *Robbery Under Arms*. Well, they are tying this in with *King Kong* and it's called *King Kong Has Rubbery Underarms*.

BARRY: They are also doing a remake of *The Hellfire Club*, *The Dambusters* and *Birth of a Nation* and they are calling it *Hellfire and Damnation*.

GRAEME: *Captain Blood* and *The Man Who Shot Liberty Valance* and they are calling it *Bloody Liberty*.

BARRY: *Up Periscope* and *Sincerely Yours* called *Sincerely Periscope*.

Tug of War

HUMPH: *Willy Rushton is the anchor man for his team, and Barry Cryer for his. They're squabbling over the rope at the moment.*
Line the hankerchief up to the centre of the page a little bit to the right – give way a little bit, Barry. Right now ... hold it, hold it. Take the strain. Now heave ...

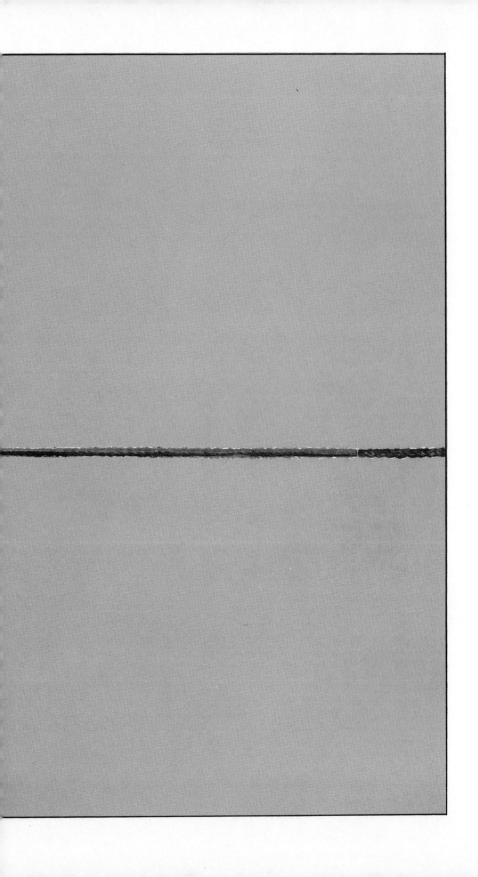

I.N.I.T.I.A.L.S.

HUMPH: *We go on to a round called 'Initials'. I'm going to read each team abbreviations, and they must tell me what they think each initial letter stands for and then I'll give them the right answer, if by any chance it differs from what they've said. Willy Rushton, the initials I want you to identify are SPCK.*

WILLY: Spitting Porridge Can Kill. It's a health warning put by the Government on.to Quaker Oats packets.

HUMPH: It doesn't look as though you're likely to win this round because that was the Society for Promoting Christian Knowledge. Barry Cryer, I'm going to go over to you now. NOSOPEX, identify that please.

BARRY: No Sopex please, we're British.

HUMPH: That's right, actually. You could have also said the Northern Sumatra Off-shore Petroleum Exploration. Tim Brooke-Taylor, here is one that you might know, this one looks a bit easy to me, BUPA.

TIM: Buried under a Pile of Aerosols. This is the British United Provident Association or something like that.

HUMPH: Very nearly. It is the British United Providence Association. I'll only dock you ten marks. Your initials, Graeme, are FHPRP.

GRAEME: It's the Faith Healers Protection Racket Practitioners. The boys who come round and lay on hands.

HUMPH: Well, it's not, actually.

GRAEME: The Foreign Hotel Proprietor's Rebuilding Programme.

HUMPH: You've got one word right, but in the wrong place. It's the Family Housing Programme Review Panel. Barry, yours is HGOA.

BARRY: Hang-gliding for the Old and Arthritic. Oh dear, I withdraw that. I'm so near to it.

TIM: You're not arthritic?

HUMPH: I'm going to tell you – it is the Houston Grand Opera Association.

BARRY: Oh, of course it is.

HUMPH: And the week's good cause now from Graeme Garden, yours is WVS.

GRAEME: WVS stands for the Association of Bad Spellers.

HUMPH: Well, yes, I suppose it does. It's also the Women's Voluntary Service.

HUMPH: Graeme, SSAFA.

GRAEME: The Society for Sending Adam Faith Away.

HUMPH: That's right. There is also a Soldiers' Sailors' and Airmen's Families' Association, but we don't want to be concerned with that.

HUMPH: Tim, your initials are DORA.

TIM: No, TBT. DORA, Des O'Connor Rites Appallingly.

HUMPH: Defence of the Realm Act. Barry Cryer, here are your initials, RTS.

BARRY: Recycle Tommy Steele. Is that right?

HUMPH: That's right. RTS could also possibly stand for Religious Tract Society ...

BARRY: No, it's not a very likely explanation.

HUMPH: Willy Rushton, NFU.

WILLY: Same to you, Norman. NFU is National Front Underwear. It's like a Y-front but more violent. The design is a target on the front, so you know where to aim, sort of underpantzers.

THE ARTISTS BALL
R. S. V. P.

Roaring in on a motorbike, with a singular lack of grace, Easel Kneasel.

With his pal, Ette.

Will you welcome, please, Mr and Mrs Madder and their daughter, Rose Madder, and her pig Ment.

Will you welcome, please, from abroad, a gentleman who not so much paints as daubs – Dauber the Greek.

Will you welcome, please, all the way from the States, Mr and Mrs Trait and their father, Por Trait.

Here with the ladies and the gents, Two Loos Lautrec, to do some impressions for us with his driver, Van Gogh.

And over there those people dressed up as parcels and letters – the post impressionists.

We just had the fancy dress competition and before the raffle the mayor will in fact light the bonfire, this is referred to in your programmes as the Pre-Raffle-Light.

The match will be drawn by Renny Sance and Len Scape.

Will you welcome, please, Mr and Mrs Ist and their son, Edward Lionel, who was recently knighted – Sir E. L. Ist.

Mr and Mrs Tomical-Drawing and their daughter, Anna Tomical-Drawing.

With their peke, Asso.

Another line of intoxicants, the Cubists.

Mr and Mrs Colours, who have descended from that well-known eighteenth-century painter, Walter Colours. (All right, we'll go quietly, Constable.)

Mr and Mrs Cturist and their daughter Carrie.

From Turkey, the Turk Wasi Blue.

MORNINGTON CRESCENT

HUMPH: *Mornington Crescent. As usual, teams, special rule applies, and that is the diagonal moves are excluded when green is faced downwards (laughs), you've got that?*

TIM: Oh, great.

GRAEME: Green is?

HUMPH: Downwards.

BARRY: Due to the demise of *Opportunity Knocks*.

HUMPH: Barry, you seem to be in good form, so you'd better start this round.

BARRY: Savile Row.

WILLY: Mornington Crescent.

BARRY: Oh God!

HUMPH: I warned you, Barry, about green being faced downwards.

TIM: You were too busy larking about with Hughie Green.

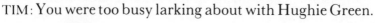

BARRY: I'm sorry, I'm sorry.

HUMPH: *Who's going to start? Willy Rushton.*

WILLY: Pembridge Crescent.

GRAEME: Queen's Park.

TIM: Oh, Willy.

WILLY: Don't blame me, do something clever.

TIM: Now you ask me!

BARRY: Come on, come on.

TIM: Regent's Park Road.

BARRY: No.

TIM: Yes, it's the South ... not the Finchley one.

GRAEME: You can't have the two – can he?

BARRY: I don't think so.

GRAEME: Not with Regent's Park.

TIM: Can I just ask – the Jubilee line we haven't brought in yet, have we?

HUMPH: Not as far as I know.

TIM: Right. Well, you're the boss. Well, I stick by it.

BARRY: Pentonville Road.

WILLY: Tooting Bec High Street.

GRAEME: Mor –

TIM: Ah ha.

GRAEME: I didn't say 'ning'.

WILLY: It's cat and mouse again.

GRAEME: I didn't get as far as 'ning'. Beak Street.

TIM: Phoenix Street.

BARRY: Albemarle Street.

WILLY: Goodge Street.

GRAEME: Mornington Crescent.

HUMPH: I could see that coming a mile off.

TIM: Be fair.

HUMPH: Well, Graeme Garden and Barry Cryer, you win that round.

AD LIB POEMS

HUMPH: *We go on now to the 'Ad Lib Poem'. As you know, this is the one where the teams make up a poem. Each team member must keep going till I press the buzzer and then a member of the opposing team must take over. This goes on until we reach a natural artistic conclusion (or the moment of truth). Barry, I'm going to give you a first line and your poem goes, 'There were two men of great renown. Their names were Tim and Willy.'*

BARRY: Who though they were in fact quite
    wise,
    Folk thought them somewhat silly
    Because they would act the fool, they
    would,
    And act the giddy goat — (BUZZER)

WILLY: One was tall, blonde, handsome,
    The other hairy throat,
    But they were so distinguished,
    The girls went mad when they
    Walked down the Mall, Park Lane,
      the Strand or even, say,
    The Balls Pond Road on Saturdays;
    You could hear at a distance shrieks —
    (BUZZER)

GRAEME: But then it kept them occupied
    For several boring weeks.
    And as these two, Willy and Tim,
    Strode out to take the air,
    The girls would point and shout at them,
    And cry out, 'We declare,
    That must be Willy, charming man,
    Pride of his whole sex' — (BUZZER)

WILLY: *Watch it!*

TIM: Hurray hurray, we all agree,
It reminds me of my old friend Tex,
All that hair upon his face,
He really looks quite pleasant,
Oh look, oh there he is walking by
Just into Mornington Crescent.

HUMPH: Well, Tim, you didn't reach an artistic conclusion, but you won the last Mornington Crescent round. So you can start another poem now, and we'll do something on a slightly different theme. 'There were two men of great renown, Graeme Garden and Barry Cryer.'

TIM: I'd say they were of great renown,
But I'm an evil liar.
G. Garden, now, he has some talent
That will I avow – (BUZZER)

BARRY: You ask him to do anything,
He always does know how.
A versatile chap, a versatile man,
Never ever confused — (BUZZER)

WILLY: He always turns the other cheek,
Whenever he's abused.
What most I like about him is
His way with the violin — (BUZZER)

GRAEME: Always on the fiddle —

WILLY: Always on the gin.

HUMPH: The first line is, 'Thirteen drunken sailors emerging from the mist'. I think we'll get Barry Cryer to start this.

BARRY: Some like Brahms and Mozart,
And some like Bach and Liszt.
They wove their way into the town
On merriment hell-bent
And found their way into a pub.
'Twas called the Duke of Kent.
'Ho there, landlord!' they all cried.
'We'll have a sup or two —' (BUZZER)

103

TIM: The first one asked for whisky,
The next a pot of glue.
'Twelve whiskies and a pot of glue,'
Cried out our bluff mine host —
(BUZZER)

GRAEME: 'I understand the whiskies,
But the glue baffles me most.'

WILLY: 'Well then,' replied one sailor.
'He normally drinks gin
But on this merry night tonight
He wants to get stuck in.'

Leaping through the door, Mr and Mrs Malfarm and their daughter Annie Malfarm.

Cock an eyebrow for Mr and Mrs Jonathan Cape and their son, the great S. Cape.

Sliding by almost unnoticed, Mr and Mrs Shonary and their diminutive student son, shorter Oxford Dick.

Will you be extremely kind and welcoming to Mr and Mrs Zeen, and their disgusting daughter Margaret – known as dirty Maggie Zeen.

Raptures of delight, if you will, for Mr and Mrs Scabin and their uncle, Tom Scabin.

Here on a day trip from France, Mr and Mrs Two Cities, and their marauding, bombastic son, Attila Two Cities.

A face unfortunately not to be seen in our midst tonight, Mr Baggers and his Carp, unfortunately, the carp ate Baggers.

Mr and Mrs Ding-Library and their son Len Ding-Library.

And who's that with them – Mr and Mrs Teasfalcon and their daughter, Moll.

Mr and Mrs Sellers, and their daughter, Bess Sellers, who's just had her appendix removed.

Oh, look, there are the Flets with their daughter, Pam.

Finally snap your garters with riddled mirth, for the entrance, all the way from France, of Mr and Mrs Misérables and their son, Les.

THE ILLUSTRATED POLICE NEWS

LAW COURTS AND WEEKLY RECORD.

INQUEST ON FIFTH VICTIM AT ST GEORGES IN THE EAST

INSPECTOR REID

FIFTH VICTIM

MORTUARY

THE BERNER ST VICTIM.

TWO MORE WHITECHAPEL HORRORS, WHEN WILL THE MURDERER BE CAPTURED ?

BACK OF BERNER STREET

POLICE CONSTABLE WATKINS SIGNALLING FOR ASSISTANCE

MITRE SQUARE ALDGATE

FATAL SPOT

THE SCENE ON SUNDAY IN BERNER STREET

FINDING THE BODY IN MITRE SQUARE.

THE FIFTH VICTIM OF THE WHITECHAPEL FIEND.

FINDING THE MUTILATED BODY IN MITRE SQARE

The Fotomas Li

MURDER

HUMPH: *We move to the game 'Murder'. This is a game which many of you have played in your stately homes. Each of the teams has to pick a card, one of which has the word 'murder' written on it. Whoever picks this is the murderer and he's then entitled to murder someone, when the lights are turned out. When there is a murder, the victim screams. I turn on the lights again and quiz, as the detective, those still surviving, in order to find the murderer. Now, after the murder, no one is allowed to move except the murderer, who is also the only person allowed to lie about his movements. Right. I will now turn out the lights.*

The Fotomas Library

IS THAT YOU DORIS?
Yes
YES HO HO!
ARRR I'VE BEEN MURDERED
TURN ON THE LIGHTS
YES TURN ON THE LIGHTS

LOOK AT THAT!
Messy
COME ON... ENOUGH IS ENOUGH TURNON THE LIGHTS
I AM THE MURDERER
GO AWAY

HUMPH: And Tim Brooke-Taylor is lying prone on the floor ... which indicates, to me at any rate, that he has been murdered. Barry, what were you doing when Tim Brooke-Taylor screamed?

BARRY: I was in the library with Miss Gussett. We had to come out. The library closes at five.

HUMPH: Right. Willy?

WILLY: I was upstairs in the bath with Penelope Keith in the blue bathroom at the end of the corridor. On hearing the scream, I made my way, with only Penelope Keith wrapped round me, to the conservatory.

BARRY: You've never liked Tim. you swine.

HUMPH: Tim, what were you doing ... oh, sorry. Graeme, I believe that you moved immediately after the scream.

GRAEME: Well, it startled me. It was a involuntary motion of the legs.

HUMPH: Where did you move to?

GRAEME: Across the room, up the stairs, down to the conservatory and on to the bus to Argentina.

HUMPH: That could be a lie, of course.

GRAEME: Would I?

HUMPH: Barry, did you see Graeme move?

BARRY: Not at first, but Miss Gussett and I met him in the Golden Egg in Buenos Aires and compared notes as to the death of Tim and decided we were both innocent. Miss Gussett held her peace and her hamburger.

HUMPH: You're all looking too innocent for me. I don't like it.

WILLY: Humph, I know this is radio, but should Tim be bleeding?

HUMPH: Willy, I'd like to ask you a question because there's something I'm particularly worried about at the moment. Who do you think did it?

WILLY: I don't know. I was giving Monty Modlyn the kiss of life at the time ... It didn't work.

ALL: It's a brave act.

HUMPH: I'll now sum up, if you'll all come into the drawing-room and sit round, I'll give you my reasons for thinking that it wasn't Graeme Garden. He was miles away at the time. It wasn't the Mystery Voice because he's asleep. I think it was Barry Cryer.

110

BARRY: Stand back, all of you.

HUMPH: Well, let's see if I'm right now. Will the real murderer please stand up. Ooooh. Good Lord, no. Well, that is a surprise.

GOOD NEWS
BAD NEWS

GRAEME: The good news is that Nicholas Parsons is retiring.

TIM: **The bad news is that he is going into show business.**

BARRY: Good news – as a human cannon-ball.

WILLY: **The bad news is, he's just been fired.**

BARRY: The good news is that there are going to be more show business personalities in the Honours List.

TIM: **Bad news – Max Bygraves is going to be knighted.**

GRAEME: Good news – now that we've leaked the news, he won't be.

WILLY: **Bad news is, he's going to be a peer instead.**

BARRY: Good news, he's standing in the sea off Bournemouth.

TIM: **Bad news – he's still singing.**

GRAEME: Good news – that'll keep the oil tankers off the rocks.

WILLY: **Bad news – Max has just slipped his moorings and is floating dangerously towards the Channel Islands.**

BARRY: Good news – the R.A.F. are hoping to disperse him with tons of underarm deodorant.

TIM: **Bad news – he's still singing.**

GRAEME: The good news is, he's just bringing out a new LP, 'Sink-along-a-Max'.

GRAEME: Good news. They've just invented a new contraceptive pill for men.

TIM: **Bad news – eight months gone and now he tells me.**

WILLY: Good news. I bought a Chinese take-away meal last night.

BARRY: **Bad news – before I could eat it, they took it away.**

TIM: Good news – half an hour later, they brought it back.

GRAEME: **Bad news – half an hour later, I brought it back.**

WILLY: Good news. I then went to a German take-away.

BARRY: **Bad news – I could only eat the food they ordered.**

TIM: Nevertheless, good news – I went to an Irish take-away.

GRAEME: **Bad news – they forgot to bring the food.**

WILLY: Good news. I didn't want soup in a basket, anyway.

BARRY: **The bad news – I then went to a Russian take-away and they took me away.**

WILLY: Good news, Enoch Powell is emigrating.

GRAEME: **Bad news, he has just been repatriated.**

TIM: Good news – he has just taken over the corner shop that stays open until ten o'clock at night.

BARRY: **Bad news – it doesn't open until five to.**

WILLY: Good news – he refuses to wear a turban on his moped.

GRAEME: **Bad news – he wears it on his head.**

113

KIM'S GAME

HUMPH: *And now we go on to a round called 'Kim's Game'. A number of items will be passed on a conveyor belt in front of one member of each team. He has to remember as many of them as possible with the help of his partner. The conveyor belt goes for ten seconds and there are thirty seconds for recollection. And the recollector can take home everything he remembers. I'm going to start with you, Tim and Willy. The objects are coming up on the conveyor belt now.*

HUMPH: Right, now you have thirty seconds for recollection.

WILLY: That woman's leg is still sticking out behind the curtain.

TIM: Cuddly toy.

WILLY: Cuddly boy.

TIM: One of those things that you plug in and you push it and it's made of solid gold and it warms the wife. And ... no! There were

two of those. Oh, there was another cuddly toy and what else, Willy?

WILLY: Larry Grayson's body.

TIM: Isla St. Clair.

WILLY: It was on the Isle of St. Clair that I met her.

TIM: Elephant foot umbrella stand.

WILLY: The elephant – on three legs.

TIM: A pair of gloves, or are those cow-warmers?

WILLY: An inebriated stagehand.

TIM: He got a fee for it, I'm happy to say.

WILLY: The man who puts the things on the end.

TIM: You can take him home.

WILLY: And a conveyor belt.

HUMPH: I worked out that you correctly recollected four items out of that, so you get four marks and you can take them back. Now before Graeme and Barry do their recollecting I would like to ask the audience not to help them because it spoils it. Graeme and Barry, here are your items on the conveyor belt, starting now.

GRAEME: Yes, Sir Charles Forte's truss.

BARRY: Fish-knives.

GRAEME: And there are some fish-plates as well … and there was the Taj Mahal by moonlight, in the wife's name.

BARRY: A see-through Labour Party.

GRAEME: A collapsible House of Commons being broadcast.

BARRY: A cuddly goy. An electric elephant.

GRAEME: Set of matching National Fronts.

BARRY: A reversible Reg Prentice.

GRAEME: The cuddly Bernard Manning.

BARRY: Impossible.

GRAEME: No, it fell off.

HUMPH: You've only got twenty-eight seconds left.

BARRY: Oh, there was a broken stopwatch. (BUZZER)

HUMPH: Barry managed to get one in there under the net, so to speak, so that puts him ahead.

HUMPH: *And the rule this time is that moves in a clockwise direction are penalized inversely.*

BARRY: Well, then, we can't win, can we?

HUMPH: Yes, you can ... moves in a clockwise direction are penalized inversely.

BARRY: I'm sorry, but I mean, it'll get you nowhere.

TIM: We can't lose, Barry.

BARRY: We can't win either.

TIM: You can go south of the river, though.

HUMPH: It's a perfectly regular and ordinary rule, Barry.

BARRY: It seems to be unfairly loaded, Humph. I'm sorry to bring this up but ...

HUMPH: Well, if you're going to sulk, you can start.

BARRY: All right . . . Oh, yes, Mornington Crescent. Ha ha ha. Yes.

TIM: No. No. No way. No good.

GRAEME: We were allowed south of the river.

BARRY: So think about it.

MORNINGTON CRESCENT

TIM: But that's not south of the river.

BARRY: No, but it's inverse.

WILLY: Ah.

HUMPH: Well, my judgement is that Barry is absolutely right, Tim and Willy, I'm afraid.

TIM: It's *not* clockwise.

HUMPH: So Barry wins that one. Well done, Barry.

TIM: It isn't clockwise. I'm sorry, it's not clockwise, Humph. You'll get letters by the million.

HUMPH: It would take too long to explain now ...

TIM: Would you please send your letters personally to Humphrey Lyttelton, not enclosing a stamped addressed envelope ... care of the Kenny Ball Memorial Home.

HUMPH: Well, as there seems to be some confusion about that game, we shall look into it and put it right and, readers, you will be notified personally.

TAG WRESTLING

HUMPH: Graeme and Barry, your punch line. *It turned out to be the female contortionist who put a ferret in the sugical boot.* Tim and Willy, here's yours: *'You've cut me off,' screamed the vicar, dismounting from his Pogo stick.'*

'You've cut me off,' screamed the vicar, dismounting from his pogo stick.

WILLY: It's a hard pogoing from the vicarage to the phone box at the bottom of the hill. But the vicar set off with some vigour down the hill towards the telephone box.

HUMPH: Graeme Garden. →

TIM: By some miracle the vicar leapt from the ditch on to his pogo stick straight towards the telephone kiosk ←

[Notice Humph always has a vicar in his stories ... Funny that ... Very Freudian ... Eton days, you know ...] Tim and Willy, you are going to start now towards your tag line ...

It turned out to be the female contortionist who put a ferret in the surgical boot.

GRAEME: Hard pogoing it was. Too hard for the vicar, who plunged from his instrument into the ditch, breaking his leg and necessitating the future wearing of a surgical boot for the rest of his days, and this story. At that moment a travelling circus appeared over the brow of the hill ... *BUZZER*

but there was a lorry coming the other way and just before he got there the lorry went across him and the vicar shouted ... **{BUZZER}** →

BARRY: The vicar shouted 'Ah!' He'd been struck a glancing blow by the lorry and fell back into the ditch right on top of a contortionist. 'Good evening, madam!!' he cried ... 'Good evening ...' **{BUZZER}**

WILLY: 'Good evening,' he said to the telephone operator as he staggered to his feet, 'I can't get through to the leg repairer.' And the next minute rather unfortunately the phone went dead and he saw ... **{BUZZER}** →

GRAEME: 'Oh, good heavens,' he said, turning to the female contortionist, 'not only have I lost the line that I was speaking on, I shall never use the telephone again in my life ...' **{BUZZER}**

TIM: But he lied ... into the phone he said, 'Can I have emergency 99 ... you've cut me off,' he said, dismounting from his pogo stick ...

HUMPH: Brilliant, I don't know how you did it.

TIM: Nor do I ...

MORNINGTON CRESCENT

A detailed analysis of the game on page 100 Careful study will enable the novice to follow the game through, move by move, and by illustration help him to improve the Tactics and Positional Play of his own game. To simplify matters, a game has been selected in which only Straight Rules (K) apply.

A typically aggressive opening by WR, although not without its perils, as it leaves his partner's South East completely exposed.

GG here follows up with a classic counter (the Luxembourg Shift), a developing move which opens all three diagonals *below the line*.

A pathetically weak response from TBT, and at this point the game is practically given away. If, instead of boxing out the F, J, O, *and* W placings he had parleyed Euston Square, this would have drawn his partners into an elliptical progression (North to South) and WR would then be in a position to take Mornington Crescent in six.

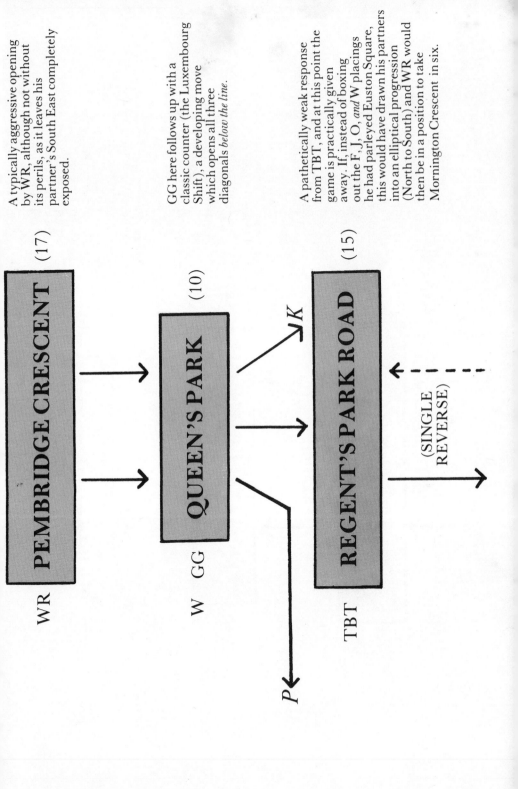

| PEMBRIDGE CRESCENT | (17) |

WR

| QUEEN'S PARK | (10) |

W   GG

K

P

| REGENT'S PARK ROAD | (15) |

TBT

(SINGLE REVERSE)

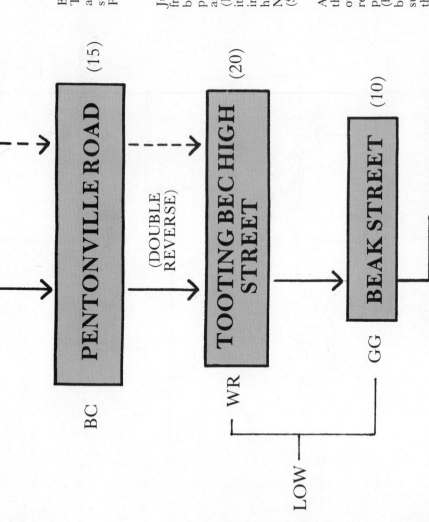

BC is quick to capitalize on TBT's weak Positional Play, and consolidates an already strong Outer Square with Pentonville Road.*

Junkin's Progression. A dangerously fragile defensive contraction, but here WR is forced to present Tooting Bec High Street as it is *the only thing he can do.* (In a Straight Rules game it is inadmissible to transfer inversely, which here would have been a powerful tactic.) Note that Q is now below (SW).

An elegant response, opening the triangle and blocking over all three possible reverse draws. Although usually played earlier in the game (before the Central Line has been quartered), GG is in such a strong position that the risk of a Terminal Move against him is negligible, as is the possibility of

PENTONVILLE ROAD (15)

(DOUBLE REVERSE)

TOOTING BEC HIGH STREET (20)

BEAK STREET (10)

(This connection is a Solitaire, as *neither*

BC

WR

GG

LOW

* Some players (including HL) favour the A40 (Northbound) here as an

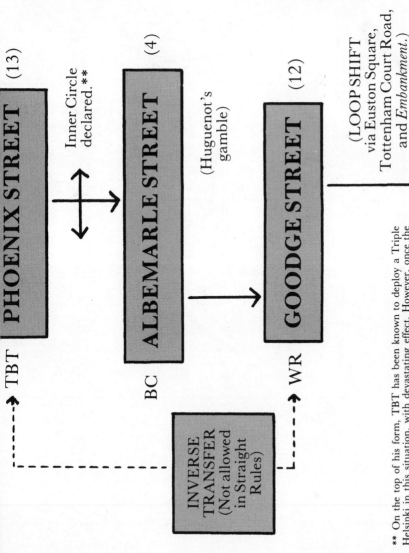

TBT seems to have given up, and his clumsy leading of Phoenix Street is pounced on by BC, whose Lateral Shift to Albemarle Street decisively breaks his opponents' vertical and horizontal approaches.

Had WR contracted Goodge Street earlier in the progression he might have opened out the game with a double Short Side. As it is, GG's sacrifice of Beak Street at a crucial intersection has led WR into the trap.

··▶ TBT

PHOENIX STREET (13)

Inner Circle declared. **

ALBEMARLE STREET (4)

BC

(Huguenot's gamble)

GOODGE STREET (12)

(LOOP SHIFT via Euston Square, Tottenham Court Road, and *Embankment*.)

··▶ WR

INVERSE TRANSFER (Not allowed in Straight Rules)

** On the top of his form, TBT has been known to deploy a Triple Helsinki in this situation, with devastating effect. However, once the Inner Circle has been declared, this move is not allowed unless *all four* players are in Fee.

↓

MORNINGTON CRESCENT (180)

GG

GG develops a curving Loop-Shift (not an easy move, and not one to be recommended to the novice and claims Mornington Crescent, thereby winning the game 40 over Base *without* Loading.

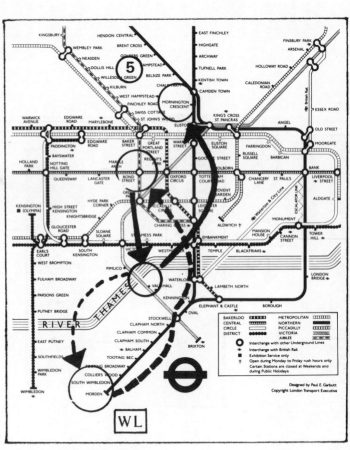

Triple Helsinki